Animal Antics

THE WINDY WHALE

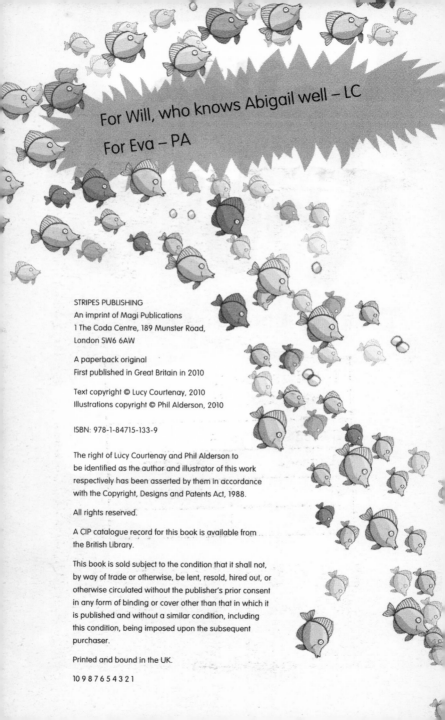

For Will, who knows Abigail well – LC

For Eva – PA

STRIPES PUBLISHING
An imprint of Magi Publications
1 The Coda Centre, 189 Munster Road,
London SW6 6AW

A paperback original
First published in Great Britain in 2010

Text copyright © Lucy Courtenay, 2010
Illustrations copyright © Phil Alderson, 2010

ISBN: 978-1-84715-133-9

The right of Lucy Courtenay and Phil Alderson to
be identified as the author and illustrator of this work
respectively has been asserted by them in accordance
with the Copyright, Designs and Patents Act, 1988.

All rights reserved.

A CIP catalogue record for this book is available from
the British Library.

Printed and bound in the UK.

10 9 8 7 6 5 4 3 2 1

Animal Antics

THE WINDY WHALE

LUCY COURTENAY

Illustrated by Phil Alderson

stripes

Animals!

Everyone loves animals. Feathery, furry, fierce. Scaly, scary, hairy. Cute, a bit smelly, all-round bonkers.

But let's be honest. How well do we really know them?
I know my dog, you might say.
I know my cat and my hamster.

Ah, I say. You may think you know them, but you DON'T.
When you watch them, they do catty
and doggy and hamstery things.
But what about when you're not watching?
Who knows what they do when you're snoozing
in your beds or when you're at school?

And what about the rest of the animal kingdom?
The world is full of amazing creatures –
from camels in the desert, to baboons
in the forest, and fish in the deepest ocean.

We know even less about them.
For all we know, they might like dancing. Or doing
handstands. Or playing thumb wars. Actually, not that
one because most animals don't have thumbs.
But you know what I mean.

Maybe we don't know animals as well as we think.
Take **WHALES** for instance…

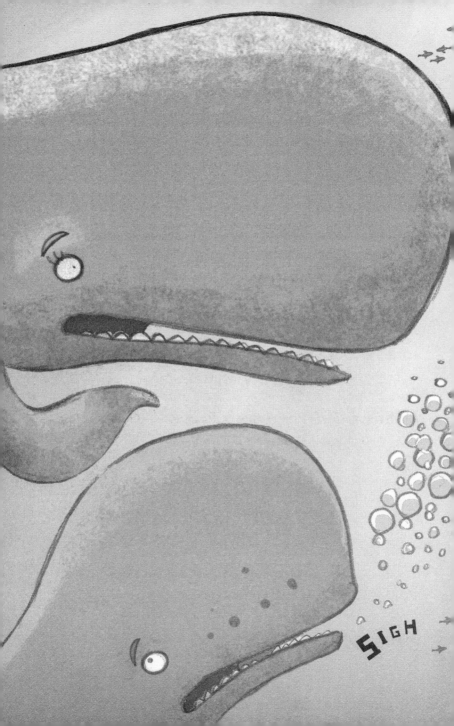

Chapter One

Abigail was the cleverest and most interesting sperm whale in her family pod, if not the whole of the Atlantic Ocean. At least, Abigail thought so. The problem was, no one else seemed to agree. Abigail couldn't understand it.

"No one EVER listens to me," she complained one dark afternoon in the depths.

"Here we go," said her brother Wayne.

Animal Antics

Wayne was older than Abigail, and made the most of it. Abigail couldn't think of a time when Wayne had ever been nice to her.

"Abigail, dear," her mother began. "We *do* listen—"

"NEVER!" said Abigail, not listening. "I've got LOTS of interesting things to say and NO ONE listens. Just yesterday, I thought of a brilliant way to catch squid and no one listened."

"We've been catching squid our way for millions of years, Abigail," said her mother. "We work in a team, herding them up. It's always worked perfectly well. Singing to them really isn't—"

"I thought of a new hunting formation you could swim in and no one listened," Abigail went on.

"It doesn't matter what shape we swim in when we're hunting," said her mother patiently. "As long as we stay close together. Besides, whales can't do rectangles—"

"AND," Abigail said, stabbing at the water with her flipper to make her point, "I thought of a fantastic way to stop barnacles from sticking to our bottoms. Why didn't anyone listen? Is it because they don't mind the barnacles? Or are they just ignoring me?"

"You're the most boring sister in the world," said Wayne. "No wonder you haven't got any friends."

Abigail gasped.

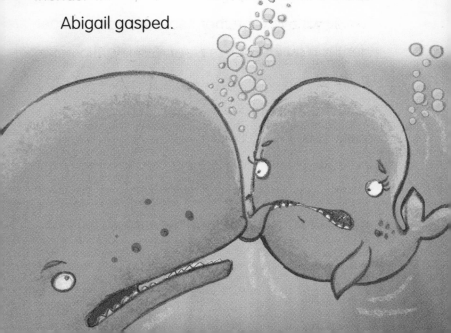

"Don't be unkind to your sister, Wayne," said Abigail's mother. "Of course she's got friends. Haven't you, Abigail?"

"Yes," said Abigail. "There's, er…"

There was a long pause. Abigail couldn't think of anyone at all.

"Well," said Abigail's mother in a bright voice, "I'm sure there are lots."

"Who are you kidding?" Wayne snorted. "No one wants to be friends with a know-it-all." And he swam off.

"Ignore your brother," said Abigail's mother gently. "You just haven't found the right whale to be friends with yet. But you do have to start listening more, Abigail, dear. You don't know everything."

Abigail felt tears popping into her eyes and mixing with the seawater. It was awful being the cleverest and most interesting whale in the pod.

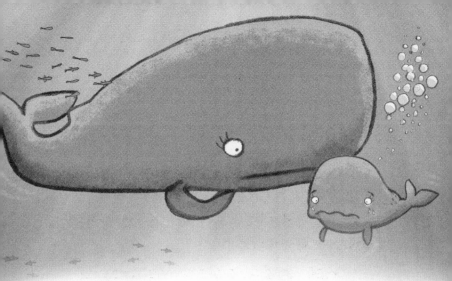

Abigail had always felt different from the other young whales. The girl whales spent all day smiling at boy whales, whilst the boy whales had competitions to see who could make the rudest noises with their blowholes. Abigail was interested in everything *except* smiling at boy whales and making rude noises. She had never minded not fitting in, because quite honestly no one else was nearly as clever or interesting as she was.

But Abigail felt something had changed. Wayne's words had hurt. Perhaps it was time

to make more of an effort to find a friend.
It wouldn't matter that they weren't as clever
or interesting as her. She had more than
enough brains to go round.

Deciding this made Abigail feel better.
Before she could change her mind, she swam
off to see what the others were doing.

The six young whales in Abigail's pod were
swimming round in circles, telling octopus
jokes. Their mothers sculled gently in the water

nearby, keeping a close eye.

"What did the girl octopus say to the boy octopus?"

"Easy. I wanna hold your hand, hand, hand, hand, hand, hand, hand, hand."

"Who holds an octopus to ransom?"

"I know this! I know this! A squidnapper!"

"What do you call an octopus with—"

"Did you know that octopi are deaf?" said Abigail, butting in.

SNIGGER!

"I don't know the answer to that one," said a small, sharp-eyed whale called Taylor.

"Hey," said a second whale called Rachel, who was larger than Taylor. "Abigail's got an octopus joke we don't know!"

All the whales looked at Abigail with interest. This was a new feeling for Abigail. They didn't usually look at her at all.

Making friends was easier than she thought.

"It's not a joke," said Abigail. "Octopi really are deaf. Isn't that a fascinating fact?"

"I've got a fascinating fact," said Wayne, swimming past with a gang of older whales. "Abigail is so boring, she sends rocks to sleep on the seabed."

"Don't be stupid, Wayne," said Abigail, as a few of the young whales giggled. "Rocks are never awake."

Wayne smirked. "Yes, they are. They just

fall asleep when they see you coming."

This made the other whales laugh even more. Abigail swam away miserably.

"Abigail?" said Taylor, following her. "Are you—"

"I expect you've got a stupid joke about me too," Abigail shouted, not listening. "Well, I think you're boring and silly and I DON'T WANT TO BE YOUR FRIEND."

Chapter Two

It's so UNFAIR, Abigail thought to herself when Taylor had gone. *I didn't ask to be clever and interesting. Why is everyone so horrible to me?*

Rachel swam over. "Are you OK, Abigail?"

"Did you think my fact about octopi was fascinating, Rachel?" Abigail asked.

"Yes," Rachel said. "But we thought it was going to be a joke."

Abigail felt furious all over again. "Why does everything have to be a joke?" she demanded.

"I didn't mean—" Rachel began.

"I know so many interesting things," Abigail went on, not listening. "And no one wants to know!"

"I *do* want to—"

"I give up," said Abigail, interrupting Rachel yet again. "I'm leaving this pod. I'm going to find a friend somewhere else."

As soon as Abigail had said this, she realized it was exactly what she needed to do. The Atlantic Ocean was massive. She was bound to find someone clever and interesting out there who wanted to listen to her and be her friend.

Turning her back on Rachel, Abigail swam over to her mother.

"Mum," she announced. "I want to leave the pod and explore the Atlantic Ocean."

Her mother looked astonished. "Leave the pod? What for?"

"To find a friend," said Abigail.

"That's very drastic, Abigail," her mother said. "Have you really tried your best to—"

"I've decided," Abigail said firmly, interrupting as usual. "Can I go?"

Her mother sighed. "You're still young and not very good at hunting for yourself," she said. "There are dangers in the Atlantic Ocean you know nothing about. There are predators and fishing fleets and—"

"I'm bigger than practically everyone else in the Atlantic Ocean, Mum," Abigail said with a laugh. "Who's going to hurt *me*?"

"It's not as easy out there as you think," said her mother.

"I'll be fine," Abigail said. "I'm clever enough to cope."

Her mother sighed. "If you want to explore the Atlantic Ocean, you can't go by yourself," she said at last. "You have to go with two friends."

Abigail shook her tail with frustration. "Haven't you been listening?" she cried. "I don't *have* any friends! That's the whole POINT!"

"Don't shout at me," said her mother. "If you want an adventure, you have to take two other whales with you. And that's that."

Abigail swam up to the surface of the Atlantic Ocean and blasted her blowhole to make herself feel better. She bashed the water with her tail and made the gulls overhead screech with fright. She couldn't see a way round her problem at all.

Animal Antics

Go exploring, but take two friends she didn't have.

Stay in the pod, but have no friends for ever.

What kind of a choice was *that*?

"Morning, Abigail, what a lovely morning it is, quite lovely, hmm?" said a grey and white seabird as it landed on Abigail's back and started pecking at the barnacles on her dorsal fin.

"Hello, Gulliver," said Abigail.

Gulliver was a smelly sort of seagull called a fulmar, and was the closest thing to a friend that Abigail had. He spoke extremely fast and often said things three times instead of once.

"How are you today, are you well, are you fine, hmm?" asked Gulliver.

Abigail shrugged.

Gulliver almost lost his footing. "Are you not well, are you poorly, are you sick, hmm?"

"Have you got any friends, Gulliver?"
Abigail asked.

The fulmar gave up on the barnacle.
"A million in my colony, is it a million, hmm?"
he said to himself between mouthfuls. "Yes,
a million, I think, a million, yes."

Abigail's eyes grew round. "You've got a
million friends?"

"I'm not friends with them all, definitely not,
no way," said Gulliver. He sneezed
seawater out of the tube-like
nostril on top of his beak.
"Nine hundred and
ninety-nine
thousand, nine
hundred and
ninety-nine of them
are idiots, fools, twits and
not my type at all, oh no."

Animal Antics

Abigail worked out the vast number in her head. "So, a million take away nine hundred and ninety-nine thousand, nine hundred and ninety-nine leaves just … you?" she said.

"Me, just me, all alone," Gulliver agreed. "Friends are dull, friends are boring, friends steal food."

"So, no friends at all then?" Abigail said, just to be sure.

"None, zero, zip," said Gulliver.

"Me neither," Abigail said glumly.

"Plenty of fish in the sea," said Gulliver. He wiped his stubby beak on Abigail's hard grey skin. "Off to catch some now, off I go, off to sea, very hungry, me."

The fulmar flew off in a flash of grey wings and a whiff of dead things. Abigail closed her blowhole and sank beneath the water again.

Plenty of fish in the sea.

Animal Antics

Gulliver was right. And it was time Abigail met a few of those fish. One of them might be her perfect friend.

But first she had to find two whales to go with her. She didn't have to be friends with them for long. When she made a *real* friend, she could swim off and lose them.

Chapter Three

It wasn't long before Abigail was back with her pod in the cool gloom of home.

The older whales were gathering for a squid hunt.

"I'm gonna get a big one," Abigail's brother Wayne chanted. "I'm gonna get a *massive* one."

The boy whales swam around the girls in high hunting spirits, telling squid jokes. The girl whales giggled and showed off their fine white teeth.

"Try singing to the squid the way I told you," Abigail told Wayne.

"Not this again," Wayne groaned.

"I worked it all out," Abigail went on. "You sing them a song and they get completely confused by the noise and then you catch them. It's just like the usual method of echolocation, only instead of making random noises you'll be more tuneful. And if you swim in a rectangular formation, you—"

"You don't know anything about squid hunts," snapped Wayne. "You've never even been on one! Leave me alone before I die of boredom, will you?"

Abigail swam away, feeling very upset. She caught Taylor looking at her. Remembering that she needed someone to explore the

Animal Antics

Atlantic Ocean with, she tried to smile.

"You should smile more often, Abigail," said Taylor. "You look much nicer when you smile."

Abigail stopped smiling at once. *Typical,* she thought. Once again, someone was out to make fun of her. Just like Wayne always did.

"Don't tell me what to do, Taylor," she said crossly.

"I didn't mean—" Taylor began.

"I can be as grumpy as I like," Abigail went on, not listening. "I don't need you to tell me when to cheer up."

Abigail's mother called for the hunters' attention. She was in charge of the hunt today. "It's time to practise our echolocation," she said. "We need to know how far away the squid are before we attack. It's dark down in the deep squid fields, and echolocation is the only way we'll find them."

"We've done echolocation *loads* of times," Wayne shouted. "Let's just go and *catch* those suckers!"

Wayne's friends cheered and high-finned Wayne on both sides.

Abigail sighed and rolled her eyes.

Animal Antics

"You'll do as you're told or you'll stay here, Wayne," Abigail's mother said, frowning.

The hunters started practising, booming and clicking at each other. The sounds echoed loudly off the nearest whales and more quietly off the ones that were further away. Wayne showed off, clicking so loudly that the noise bounced off four whales and a passing manta ray, confusing everyone completely.

"Your brother's an idiot, isn't he, Abigail?" said Rachel.

Abigail looked at Rachel in astonishment. Finally, a whale in her pod had said something *sensible*.

"Yes," she said. "He is."

She smiled at Rachel. Rachel smiled back.

Abigail knew it was now or never.

"Do you want to explore the Atlantic Ocean with me, Rachel?" she asked.

"OK," Rachel said. "But only if I get to tell the jokes and Taylor comes too."

Abigail's heart sank. "Taylor?" she said. "Why Taylor?"

"Because she's my friend," said Rachel. "And if you want me to come, Taylor has to come as well."

Abigail sighed. She wasn't keen on Taylor coming, but it didn't look like she had a choice.

"Taylor?" Abigail called over as graciously as she could. "Rachel and I are going to explore the Atlantic Ocean and Rachel wants you to come too."

"Great!" said Taylor, swimming over to join them.

"Why do you want to explore the ocean anyway, Abigail?" asked Rachel.

"There are lots of interesting things out there," said Abigail, waving a flipper at the deep blue water all around. "I don't want to spend all my life in one pod. I want to meet new creatures and see new things." *And find a friend*, she added to herself.

"I'd like to see some angelfish," said Taylor. "They're supposed to be really pretty."

"They live in coral, don't they?" said Rachel. "I've heard that coral is great to scratch your tummy on."

"So you'll check with your mums tonight?" Abigail asked. "I want to leave tomorrow."

Taylor and Rachel nodded.

"Atlantic Ocean, here we come!" said Abigail in triumph.

Chapter Four

Abigail, Taylor and Rachel gathered on the surface of the Atlantic Ocean at sunrise the following morning. One half of the fiery orange sun shimmered behind a bank of clouds on the horizon. The other half was still out of sight.

Abigail had never seen the sunrise before. She dipped her head below the water for a few minutes, then lifted it up again.

"What were you looking for?" asked Rachel.

"The rest of the sun," Abigail explained.

Taylor giggled.

"What are you laughing at?" Abigail asked.

"The rest of the sun isn't *in* the sea," said Taylor.

"Of course it is," said Abigail. "It's not on top of the sea, is it?"

"Well, no—" Taylor began.

"So therefore it's *in* the sea," said Abigail, as patiently as she could.

Before Taylor could argue, Gulliver flapped out of the sky and landed on Abigail's head.

"What a gorgeous sunrise, indeed, the colours of fire, hmm?" the fulmar said.

"Gulliver," said Abigail. "The sun rises out of the sea in the morning, doesn't it?"

Gulliver cracked his beak. "Don't ask me, no idea, not a clue."

Animal Antics

"It doesn't," said Taylor.

"It DOES," said Abigail.

"You found some friends, Abigail, hmm?" Gulliver said, looking at Taylor and Rachel with interest. "Look like friends to me. Quibble quabble, squibble squabble." He did one of his seawater sneezes, then swooped off calling,

"TOODLE-OO, TOODLE-PIP, TOODLE-SQUEAK."

Animal Antics

"It's silly arguing when we've only just set off," said Rachel, as they watched Gulliver fly away.

"I agree," said Taylor.

"I suppose," said Abigail grumpily.

"I've got a good joke," said Rachel. "What do you call a fish with no eyes?"

"No eye-dea," said Taylor, and giggled.

Abigail forgot to be grumpy. She wanted to know the answer to Rachel's joke.

"A blindfish?" she guessed.

Rachel grinned. "A fsh."

A smile tugged at the corner of Abigail's mouth. Rachel could be pretty funny sometimes.

They swam eastwards. To Abigail's disappointment, there was no sign of the sun in the sea. When they came up for air, the sun hung in the sky like a golden flatfish, with nothing left beneath the water at all.

Gulliver the fulmar was waiting.

"Hello, Abigail and friends," he said, settling comfortably on Abigail's back. "So friendly, still together, lovely."

Abigail decided not to argue. It had been nice swimming with Taylor and Rachel after all. "Are you following us, Gulliver?" she asked.

"Very nice, flat, comfy to sit on you," Gulliver said. "And I have news, facts, information." He slapped his large webbed feet up and down on Abigail's back. "I asked my colony about the sun, hmm, lots of questions. The sun doesn't live in the sea at night time, oh no. It never sleeps, not a wink, not a snore. It keeps moving, over sea, over land, always daylight somewhere, hmm?"

Abigail stared. "Are you sure?"

"As sure as a million fulmars who fly in the sun all day, certain, positive, oh yes. Bye now, bye bye bye."

The fulmar shook his feathers and took off into the brightening sky.

But I'm never wrong, Abigail thought. *Am I?*

For the first time in her life, Abigail felt uncertain.

"Abigail?" said Rachel. "Do you want to say something to Taylor?"

Abigail had never apologized to anyone before. She squirmed and wriggled. "Um," she said at last.

"I think Abigail is trying to say sorry," Rachel told Taylor. "Aren't you, Abigail?"

"Yes," Abigail muttered. "Sorry."

"Don't worry about it, Abigail," Taylor said. "It was an easy mistake to make."

Animal Antics

They dipped beneath the waves again and swam on. Abigail was unusually quiet. Discovering that she'd been wrong was a terrible shock.

Chapter Five

For a few hours, the three whales saw nothing at all.

"I'm bored," Taylor said, the next time they came up for air. "Where is everyone? I thought we'd have seen some exciting creatures by now."

"We've only been gone for half a day," said Abigail. Her confidence was back. "We haven't reached the interesting bit of the Atlantic Ocean yet."

"How do you know?" Taylor asked.

"How old are you, Taylor?" Abigail asked in her most patient voice.

"Six," said Taylor.

"How old are you, Rachel?" Abigail continued.

"Six and a half," said Rachel.

"Well, I'm seven," said Abigail, "so I know more than you." She peered through the water. "Look," she said in triumph. "There's something interesting over there. I'll go and say hello."

A sleek shape was gliding through the water towards them. It had a long pointed nose and stripes down its body.

"I think that's a tiger shark," said Rachel suddenly. "Don't go any closer, Abigail. It might eat—"

But Abigail wasn't listening.

"Hello," she said, swimming towards the shark and wearing her best smile. "I like your stripes. What are you, then?"

"Well, hello," the shark purred back. His teeth gleamed in the blue water. "What am I? Just a fish, really. A stripey, friendly sort of fish. What a lovely smile you have, my dear."

Animal Antics

Abigail blushed with pride. Ignoring Taylor and Rachel's frantic calls, she swam a little closer.

"You're a very big fish," she said.

The shark twitched its tail. "I suppose I am," he said. "Mainly thanks to … *stupid young whales like you.*"

His teeth flashed into the space where Abigail's nose had been. Abigail jerked back in shock. She half-turned as he lunged again. This time his teeth connected with her side.

"OW!" Abigail squealed.

Suddenly, Taylor and Rachel were beside her. The water boiled and churned as they hit the tiger shark with their tails and nipped at his belly.

"Take that, Stripey!"

"And that!"

"Hey!" protested the shark. "Three against one's not fair!"

"Swim away, Abigail!" Taylor yelled. "There'll be more sharks in a minute. They love the smell of blood."

"Go, Abigail!" shouted Rachel. "Go!"

Abigail forced her terrified flippers to work. But in her panic, she shot towards the shark by mistake. Her huge head connected with the tip of his nose. This time it was the shark's turn to yell with pain.

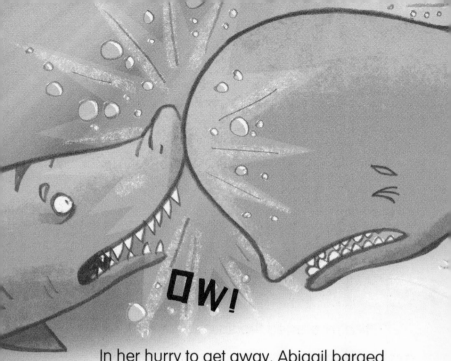

OW!

In her hurry to get away, Abigail barged into Taylor, then bumped into Rachel. The three whales scrambled for clear water, and the tiger shark was swallowed up in the gloom.

"Thanks," Abigail panted. Her flank stung where the shark had bitten her. She felt embarrassed and stupid. "I think you just saved my life. I thought it looked friendly!"

"Mum warned me about sharks," said Rachel.

"I expect your mum warned you about them too," Taylor added.

Had her mum warned her? Abigail couldn't remember. Then again, she never remembered much of anything her mother said.

"Well, thanks again," she said humbly.

"No problem," said Taylor. "But Abigail? Will you do us a favour?"

"Of course," said Abigail. She was desperate to show Rachel and Taylor how grateful she was. "Anything."

"Can you listen to us?" Taylor said.

Abigail frowned in confusion. "What?"

"You never listen," said Taylor. "You didn't listen when I asked if you were OK that time your brother was horrible to you. You didn't listen when I told you that you had a nice smile. You didn't listen when I told you the sun didn't live in the sea."

"And you didn't listen when we warned you about the shark," Rachel added.

Abigail felt embarrassed all over again. Her mum was always telling her to listen. But she hadn't listened.

"You think I've got a nice smile?" she said at last.

"Yes," said Taylor.

"And you weren't coming to tease me about my fascinating octopus fact?" Abigail checked.

"Why would I do that?" Taylor said.

"I thought it was quite interesting," said Rachel.

"Me too," Taylor agreed. "So, will you listen to us more in future?"

Abigail smiled tentatively. Taylor and Rachel smiled back.

"OK," Abigail said. "I'll try."

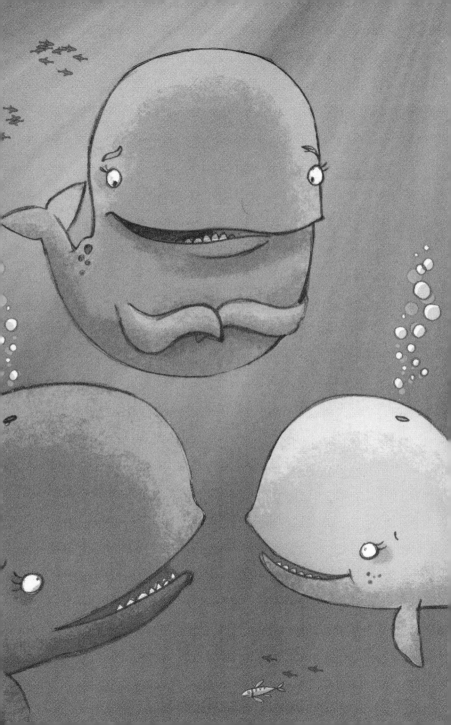

Chapter Six

Abigail did her best to listen to Taylor and Rachel and not say anything at all for the next hour. It was very difficult, but Abigail discovered Taylor and Rachel both knew things that were worth listening to.

Taylor loved anything that was pretty, and knew about the sun and the seasons. Abigail had never really thought about the seasons

before. She'd just accepted that the water was
cold on some days and warmer on others.
Rachel knew some great jokes and lots of
funny songs, including one called *A Whale
Robbed A Snail*.

A WHALE ROBBED A SNAIL IN A HOWLING GALE,
HOWLING GALE, HOWLING GALE,
A WHALE ROBBED A SNAIL AND THE SNAIL DID WAIL,
SO THE WHA-HALE WENT TO JAIL!

Animal Antics

They sang it in a round, over and over again, swapping their names for the whale and the snail as they went along and laughing so much they swallowed half the Atlantic. To her amazement, Abigail found that she was enjoying herself.

They were far away from home now. Seaweed floated on the surface, which meant the water was getting shallower.

"Wow!" Taylor gasped, as a bright yellow shoal of fish glided by. "I've never seen fish like that before. Aren't they lovely?"

Animal Antics

"Do you think we can eat them?" asked Rachel. "I'm starving."

"You should never eat fish you don't recognize," Abigail said. "They might be poisonous."

"Abigail's right," said Taylor. "We should stick to squid."

"I can't see any squid," Rachel sighed.

"Let's play chase to take our minds off food," Abigail suggested. She flipped her tail and darted ahead of the others. "Can't catch me!" she called over her shoulder.

Taylor and Rachel chased her through the blue waves. Abigail was a strong swimmer, but so were the others. Breathless and laughing, the three whales headed up for air.

In the distance, a long, dark shape lay close to the horizon.

"Is that *land*?" said Taylor.

Animal Antics

"I've never seen land," Rachel gasped.

Abigail had never seen land either. "Let's go closer," she said in excitement.

Taylor and Rachel hung back.

"My mum said never to get too close to land," Taylor said. "There might be *whalers*."

Animal Antics

The word sent a shiver down Abigail's spine. Like all young whales, Abigail had heard the stories. Whalers came in big ships and killed whales with long, sharp sticks. Whalers rounded up whales with loud horns and clattering drums, and drove whales ashore to die. Whalers turned the seawater red with blood.

"Whalers?" said Rachel in a faint voice. "I don't want to meet any whalers."

"Me neither," said Taylor.

Abigail looked at the water that lay between them and the land. Her perfect friend could still be waiting for her out there.

"I've come this far," she said. "I'm not turning round now."

"We've seen beautiful fish, met a tiger shark and seen land," Taylor said in surprise. "What more do you want to do?"

Animal Antics

"I want to find a friend," said Abigail.

"But I thought we were your—" started Taylor.

"I've never had a friend," confessed Abigail.

"But *we're* your—" said Rachel.

"I came on this expedition to find one," Abigail continued. "So that's what I'm going to do. But you don't have to stay."

She was surprised by how sad she felt at the thought of Taylor and Rachel going home without her.

"OK," said Taylor after a minute. "If that's what you want. But we *are* your—"

"Thanks for coming this far with me," said Abigail. She touched flippers awkwardly with Taylor and Rachel. "Hope you get home OK. And don't let my mum tell you off for leaving me behind."

And she ducked down under the water to swim towards the shore.

Chapter seven

The water was growing lighter and bluer and warmer. Abigail kept swimming, looking for someone to talk to. It felt strange being all on her own. Everything was very quiet without Taylor and Rachel.

She saw a ray flying through the water up ahead.

"Excuse me?" she called.

Animal Antics

The ray flicked its long tail. "What do you want?" it said suspiciously.

Abigail eyed the spike on the ray's tail. "Nothing," she said, backing away. "Sorry I disturbed you."

She swam closer to shore. When she came up to breathe, she checked the horizon nervously for whalers. The only things she saw were birds bobbing on the water, their sharp beaks flashing down into the sea and pulling up fish.

Abigail's tummy rumbled. She'd had nothing to eat all day. She glanced around hopefully for squid. Suddenly, bright fish darted beneath her belly, startling her.

"Taylor!" she called, forgetting that she was on her own. "Look! Angelfish!"

There was silence. Feeling silly, Abigail swam on.

The next thing she saw was coral. She scratched her tummy on it and grunted with pleasure. It was a gorgeous feeling.

Rachel would love this, she thought.

But Rachel wasn't there either.

Abigail started to feel rather lonely.

She could see seagrass growing on the seabed now, waving gently in the current. Moving through the grass was something large and pale, with a whiskery face and two stubby flippers. Abigail checked for sharp teeth or poisonous spikes, but couldn't see any.

"Hello?" she said.

The creature blinked at her, its mouth full of seagrass. It was very odd. It reminded Abigail of a whale or a dolphin, but it was standing on its tail.

"What are you?" said Abigail curiously.

"What are *you*?" said the creature.

Animal Antics

"I'm a sperm whale," said Abigail.

Suddenly she realized what kind of animal she was looking at. She'd heard about them from her mum.

"You're a manatee!" she said.

The manatee nodded.

"Is that nice?" asked Abigail, looking at the grass.

Animal Antics

The manatee waved a flipper, inviting Abigail to eat.

"I've never eaten grass before," said Abigail. "Does it taste good?"

"Good," said the manatee. She waved her flipper at the grass again.

Abigail was so hungry that she decided to try it. The grass was slippery and salty and reminded her of squid tentacles, but without the squiddy taste. She smiled at the manatee. The manatee smiled back.

Animal Antics

Maybe this is the friend I've been looking for! Abigail thought.

"Would you like to be my friend?" she asked shyly, between mouthfuls.

"Would you like to be *my* friend?" the manatee replied.

Abigail felt a rush of delight. This was *exactly* how making friends should be. No arguing. No disagreements.

I'm so glad I came on this trip, she thought happily.

"What's your name?" she asked. "I'm Abigail."

The manatee smiled. "*I'm* Abigail," she said.

"We've got the same name!" Abigail gasped, unable to believe her luck. "We're *definitely* meant to be friends!"

She studied the manatee. "How do you balance on your tail like that?" she asked.

"Is it comfortable? I'm going to try it."

She dipped her tail down and settled it in the middle of the grass. It felt strange.

"Is this right?" Abigail checked.

The manatee nodded.

"I can see we're going to be best friends,"
said Abigail, giving the manatee a huge smile.

"Best friends," repeated the manatee,
smiling back.

Abigail couldn't remember feeling so happy.
The manatee was interested in everything she
said, and smiled at her the whole time. Abigail
chattered away, eating as she went. The taste
of seagrass was growing on her.

"So I thought singing at the squid was a
brilliant idea, because they'd be totally
confused by the noise and we could catch
them easily," she told her new best friend.

"Easily," nodded the manatee.

"But no one agreed," Abigail sighed. "They
ought to meet you, Abigail. You agree with
everything I say."

Animal Antics

Abigail the manatee nodded.

"And then there was this fantastic idea I had about the barnacles," Abigail continued.

"Barnacles?"

"They always grow on our bottoms," Abigail explained. "It gets a bit uncomfortable."

The manatee nodded, encouraging Abigail to go on.

Abigail was in raptures. She'd never met such a friendly creature in her whole life. "So I had this bright idea," she went on, and told her new friend all about it.

The manatee nodded, and munched more grass, and nodded again.

"But no one listened," Abigail finished gloomily. "They've got no imagination."

"No imagination," agreed the manatee.

Abigail gazed at the beautiful seagrass bed, the pretty fish swimming overhead and the admiring face of Abigail the manatee.

"I want to stay here for ever," said Abigail
impulsively.

The manatee beamed at her. "For ever,"
she said.

BuRP!

Chapter Eight

After two days, Abigail's tail started to hurt. Her tummy was feeling rather odd as well. She gave it a rub and burped by mistake.

"Oh," she said, feeling embarrassed. "Excuse me, Abigail."

The manatee stopped chewing. "Excuse me, Abigail," she said, smiling.

"No," Abigail said with a laugh, "you don't

have to say excuse me. I did the burp."

"*I* did the burp," the manatee corrected.

Abigail stared. The burp had definitely been hers. She'd felt it bubbling up her throat. "No, it was *me*," she said.

"No," said the manatee. "It was *me*."

Abigail was confused. They were arguing about who had burped?

"Forget it," she said after a moment.

Her tail really was hurting. She flipped it up and waved it in the current. "That is so much better," she sighed.

"Much better," agreed the manatee.

Abigail looked uncertainly at her new friend. Sometimes it felt like the manatee was just repeating everything she said. Then she gazed at the seagrass. She wasn't sure she could eat much more of it.

"What else do you do around here?"

The manatee stared at her as if she hadn't understood the question.

"Oh," said Abigail, settling her tail down again. "You mean, you just eat?"

The manatee smiled, and chewed on a tendril of seagrass. Abigail suddenly realized she was bored. Totally and completely bored. She missed Taylor and Rachel. She missed her mum. Most amazing of all, she even missed Wayne.

Animal Antics

"Listen," she said. "You're really nice and everything, but I think I have to go now. I'm not very good at being a manatee really."

"Really?" said the manatee.

"Really," Abigail said. "It was lovely meeting you. Keep, er ... keep eating. Bye."

And she swam away, back into the inviting blueness of the deep, dark Atlantic Ocean.

Oh, the glory of swimming home! Abigail revelled in it. She squirmed with pleasure as the water grew colder against her skin. She avoided the waters where they had met the tiger shark, and flipped her tail with delight each time she rose to the surface. She hoped Taylor and Rachel had got home OK. She couldn't wait to tell them about Abigail the manatee.

Animal Antics

As the day wore on, Abigail's tummy started to make strange rumbling sounds. She pressed on as best she could, but she was feeling more and more uncomfortable.

When she broke the surface for the fourth time, there was a flapping noise above her head. Gulliver the fulmar landed on her back.

Animal Antics

"Abigail, trouble, trouble, trouble," he gabbled. He spoke even more quickly than usual. "So much trouble, awful, dreadful, help!"

Abigail's stomach lurched and rumbled. "What are you talking about, Gulliver?" she said, trying to ignore her belly.

The fulmar was so agitated he sneezed twice. "Ships, boats, vessels," he shouted, spraying smelly seawater everywhere. "Sharp sticks, oh so sharp, calamity!"

This time, the lurch in Abigail's stomach had nothing to do with the seagrass. "Sharp sticks?" she said. "Ships? Gulliver, you're not talking about – *whalers*, are you?"

"Go quick, fast as fast as fast!" Gulliver screeched. "They are coming, moving, sailing close!"

He took off in a whirl of feathers, his big feet flailing in the air. Abigail stared in terror at the outline of a large ship sailing almost out of sight ahead of her – straight towards the part of the ocean where her family lived.

She plunged back beneath the water.

She had to warn the pod!

RUMBLE! RUMBLE!

Chapter Nine

Abigail drove forward as hard as she could, but her flippers felt tired and sluggish. Her tummy rumbled and roared in protest. It felt like she was hardly moving. She bobbed to the surface to see the whaling ship still steaming ahead, greasy smoke blowing from its funnel.

In horror, Abigail realized she didn't have enough strength to swim faster. She wasn't designed to eat seagrass. She was designed to eat squid.

Like a miracle, she saw a small squid scooting along in the water a short distance away.

I'll sing A Whale Robbed A Snail *to it*, Abigail thought, suddenly fired with hope. *I'll confuse it and catch it and get strong enough to reach my family before the whalers get there.*

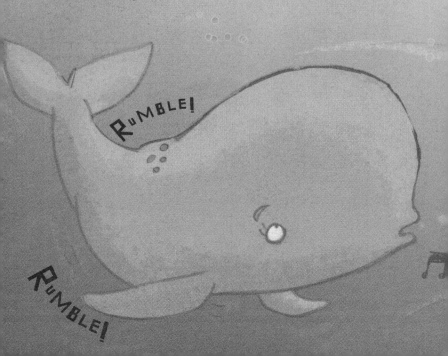

Animal Antics

"A whale robbed a snail in a howling gale," she began to sing.

BAAOOW went her tummy like it was trying to sing along.

"Howling gale, howling gale," Abigail sang.

BAAOOUUEE sang her stomach.

The squid caught sight of her. It shot off into the darkness, gone from sight for ever. Abigail felt shocked. Why hadn't it worked? She'd been so *sure*...

Animal Antics

A little voice niggled in her head. *If octopi are deaf, squid are probably deaf too.*

BRUMP went her tummy. She groaned, feeling ill *and* unhappy now. What an idiot she was. No wonder Wayne thought she was such a loser.

I'm not clever, she thought in despair. *I'm stupid and thoughtless and I never listen when it matters. I shouldn't have wasted my time on manatees and seagrass. I should have gone home with Taylor and Rachel. We could have faced the whalers together. We could have been friends.*

BLOOPBLOPBROP...

Abigail forced her flippers to work harder. She was gaining on the whalers, but slowly. Too slowly.

Abigail thought hopelessly about all the stupid things she'd done and daft ideas she'd had. The barnacle idea was still good, but the memory of everything else stabbed her like a whaler's harpoon. She vowed to make it up to everyone – if only she could make it home in time.

She could see the underside of the whaling ship now. It was rusty and covered in more barnacles than she had ever seen. She ducked down deep so that the whalers wouldn't see her.

Her chest began to feel tight. She only had a few minutes left before she had to breathe. She needed to get past the ship before she could surface. She was too weak to click or boom a warning, but she could feel her family nearby.

"HURGH!" she groaned, making one last huge effort.

BRAAOOWARGH growled her stomach.

And the most gigantic fart the Atlantic Ocean had ever heard shot out of Abigail's bottom.

BOOOOOOOM!

Chapter Ten

The great ball of gas ballooned in the water and shot upwards like an erupting volcano. Abigail was knocked sideways by the force of it. There was a boom and a shudder somewhere above her as the fart broke the surface.

She gazed cautiously up as the water boiled and shook and shimmered. She felt a hundred times better, but also a hundred

times worse. She'd lost sight of the whalers.
She felt so dreadful about her family that
she wanted to sink until her belly touched
the seabed. But her body had different
ideas. Her flippers paddled and her tail
dipped up and down, bringing her to the
surface to breathe.

Abigail reached the choppy surface with
seconds to spare. She opened her blowhole,
gasped for air and choked. The smell was
terrible. Panicking, she looked for the whaling
ship, but it was nowhere in sight.

"What a stink, a pong, a whiff," said
Gulliver cheerfully, landing on Abigail's head.

"Gulliver," Abigail sobbed. "Where's the
ship? Did they get my family?"

"Oh no, all wrong, mistaken entirely,"
Gulliver said. "Have a look, can you see, can
you tell, hmm?"

He lifted a wing and
pointed. Abigail turned.
Behind her, something
that looked like a ship
was sticking oddly
out of the water, its
prow pointing at the sky.
Yells and shouts floated
across the waves.

"What happened?" Abigail said in
confusion.

The surface erupted again as Abigail was
surrounded by her pod. Everyone gasped at
the smell. Gulliver shrieked and flew off
Abigail's back before he got washed away.

"Abigail, it *is* you!" Taylor cried. "We saw
you coming, but then the water exploded."

"Hi, Abigail!" Rachel said in excitement.
"Welcome back!"

Animal Antics

"Abigail, dear!" Abigail's mother folded Abigail in her flippers. "I'm so glad you're home safe. Whatever was that noise? And is that a whaling ship sinking behind you?"

Abigail gazed at the remains of the whaling ship. Only the prow could still be seen. A little boat filled with men had started rowing slowly away from the wreckage.

Suddenly, she understood what had happened.

"I sank the whalers!" she gasped.

"Oh, Abigail," said her mother, "it's good to have you home, but it was an underwater volcano or a tsunami or something that sank that ship. I hardly think—"

"I *did*!" Abigail said, blushing. "I farted and I blew them out of the water and they sank."

"Seriously?" said Wayne. He looked at Abigail in awe. "Because you *farted*?"

Animal Antics

Abigail told them about her three days of seagrass. Rachel guffawed.

"I thought it smelt a little odd up here," said Abigail's mother.

"More than odd," said Wayne. "Totally disgusting. Good one, sis!"

"I've been an idiot," Abigail confessed. "I'm really sorry for never listening and for going on about my stupid ideas and never hearing anyone else's opinion. My Atlantic Ocean expedition has taught me a lesson."

Her mother smiled at her. Her neat white teeth gleamed in the sunshine. "And did you find a friend?" she asked.

Abigail thought about the boring manatee. She didn't dare to look at Taylor or Rachel. "No," she said sadly.

Taylor touched her with a flipper. "Yes, you did, Abigail," she said. "You found two."

Animal Antics

"You're an idiot who never listens to a word we say, but we like you," Rachel added. "Especially now, Miss Fartyflippers."

"Ah friends, mates, chums," shouted Gulliver, wheeling high in the sky as Abigail giggled and blushed and smiled at everyone until her jaw ached. "They steal your food, call you names, tell bad jokes, no good, no good at all. Off to catch some fish now, lovely guts, stinky scales, all for me!"

Just a bit left...

All was peaceful in the seagrass beds.

Makini the manatee hummed quietly to herself, letting the current tickle her under the flippers as she ate. She couldn't help feeling relieved that the odd grey monster had gone at last.

She hadn't understood a word it said.

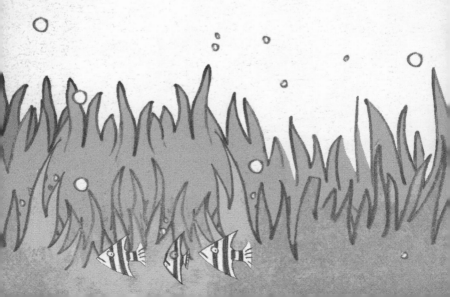

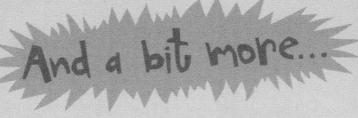
And a bit more...

"I know this sounds mad," said the whaling captain as his men rowed the lifeboat towards the sunset, "but that explosion smelled like a fart."

"It wasn't me, captain," said the first mate.

"Me neither!"

"Nor me!"

THE END

Totally True

Fulmars are named after two Old Norse words: *full* meaning foul and *mar* meaning gull. They really do pong.

The manatee's closest living relative is the elephant.

No one knows what a sperm whale's teeth are for, as they aren't used to eat with. Perhaps they really are for smiling.

The sperm whale has the largest brain of any known animal. So Abigail *is* one of the cleverest things in the sea. But not even she knows how to get barnacles off anything.

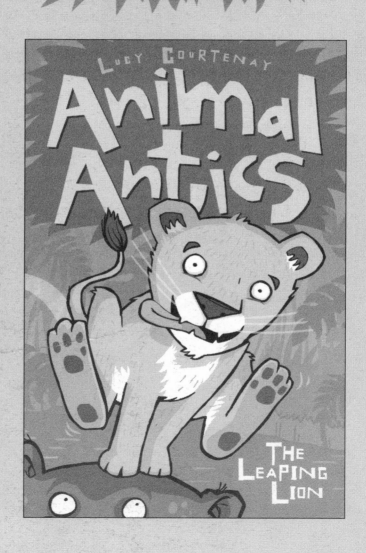

LUCY COURTENAY

Animal Antics

THE
LEAPING
LION

Brian the lion is small and springy, and loves to leapfrog. He's leaped over hyenas and zebras and all the rocks on the savannah. But now he's looking for something even bigger.

Surely Big Earl the bull elephant won't mind being Brian's Perfect Leapfrog Challenge…

Coming soon:

Animal Antics

THE POTTY PENGUIN